Praise for Alain Elkann's Anita!

"Elkann's book envelopes and hypnotizes you with words after a prelude similar to a plane waiting for the green light from the control tower."

Claudio Baroni, *Corriere della Sera*

"If you believe the publisher i.e., the title, the cover layout, the blurb, it's a romance novel. If you believe me, who has read the text enclosed within this romantic wrapping, it is a book about the dilemma, if not about the diatribe, cremation/burial."

Camillo Langone, *il Giornale*

"Alain Elkann takes [death] head-on and addresses it on virtually every page of this book. He tells us about his own death. Not just other people's. And he does so with an enviable ease, with a subtle, disorienting sense of humor. He mocks us and himself, as when he discovers that he slept for months with his girlfriend but also with the ashes of her mother, placed in a box in the bedroom, in plain sight."

Elena Loewenthal, *Il Foglio*

CROSSINGS 32

ALSO BY ALAIN ELKANN IN ENGLISH

Piazza Carignano (1985)
Misguided Lives (1989)
Moravia (2000)
Envy (2007)
The French Father (2012)
The Voice of Pistoletto (2014)
Alain Elkann Interviews (2017)
Money Must Stay in the Family (2018)

Anita

ANITA

A novel

Alain Elkann

Translation by
K.E. Bättig von Wittelsbach

BORDIGHERA PRESS

Library of Congress Control Number: 2021947116

Cover Art: Alex Katz

Printed in the United States.

Published by
BORDIGHERA PRESS
John D. Calandra Italian American Institute
25 West 43rd Street, 17th Floor
New York, NY 10036

CROSSINGS 32
ISBN 978-1-59954-170-9

Table of Contents

TRANSLATOR'S NOTE

For their friendship, wisdom, and kindness, the translator warmly thanks Wayles Browne, David DeVries, Alain Elkann, Michael Pastore, Anthony Julian Tamburri, and Etienne Wagnière.

She dedicates this translation to her students at Cornell University.

Anita

My name is Milan because my mother adored books by Milan Kundera. But since her brother, named Misha, had been killed in a concentration camp, my mother always called me Misha and that is how I became Misha for everyone. My name can be written in many different ways, depending on the language. I prefer to write it as Misha.

That said, for many days now I've been considering writing down a series of facts that made me think about the consequences of my death. Yet, to do so I should first say something about the path that led me to the thoughts that I am about to write down.

If one could turn back and rewrite one's life, I would have wanted to meet Anita when we were young....

She played tennis dressed in white with a Dunlop Maxply racket, on a red clay court among the pine trees in Forte dei Marmi. She had arrived at the Tennis Club on a bike, a blue *Bianchi*. On the handlebar hung a straw basket where she would place a racket and a box of balls. She wore short white socks, a pair of white Superga shoes, a white skirt, a white tee-shirt. A pale-yellow cardigan was tied around her neck, falling around her shoulders. After a match, she stopped in a café with a girlfriend, lit a cigarette, a Muratti Ambassador, and sat down to drink a Coke with ice and lemon. Anita was a nineteen-year-old French girl, on vacation with her sister Anne and their mother. They stayed at the *Hotel Augustus* and went to swim at the *Bagni Piero* Beach Club. In the evening Anita and her sister would go to *La Capannina* to dance and flirt with two Italian youths: Anita with a boy from Venice, Anne with a Florentine. Sometimes they went to an open-air cinema. Film was of no interest to them, but kissing and being kissed by their boys was. After the movies they would stop at a Venetian-style ice cream shop to buy a cone. Anita's was almost always a chocolate one and Anne preferred a *stracciatella.* How lovely those long July days were, that atmosphere between the beach and the pines! Mary, the mother, had friends and they played bridge together. She spent little time on the beach, and grudgingly, because she did not like to swim and could not stand the sun. In the evening she was always elegant, coming down to the café terrace for a drink before dinner. Mary was proud of her girls, because they were beautiful, young, long-limbed, and she knew that at night they secretly went to dance until dawn and that one should not wake them up in the morning. When Jean, her husband, arrived for the long weekend of July 14th, Mary acquired a gentler smile, because although Jean would spend a long time swimming, and joked with the daughters, she felt that he was there because of her. There was something special in that month of July in Forte dei Marmi, a sort of truce that would not last long. Mary was very aware of this: the times had changed, the girls were grown-up, they would leave home, get married, her own husband would grow old and stop swimming, and she would be left alone.

I imagined that I could have met Anita at *La Capannina* or during an afternoon of tennis. After some shy first moves, we would have kissed, and our lives would be changed. We would have our ups and downs, I would go visit her in Paris and then we would spend a vacation together, in the mountains. We were still students, but after university I would find a job in a New York publishing house, and we would write each other many letters and make long phone calls. In America I would court other girls, and in Paris she would have other affairs.

One day, I would be in the office, and the phone would ring.

"It's me."

"Anita?"

"Yes, I am in New York. I've been here for a week and I feel like seeing you."

"Are you alone?"

"No, I came here with a friend, but he is leaving tomorrow, and I am staying for a few more days."

"Wonderful. Let's meet whenever you like."

"Lunch the day after tomorrow at *Sant'Ambroeus*? Is that all right?"

"Great."

"At one?"

"Yes, sure."

"A kiss, then."

"To you, too."

I would have been excited to meet Anita: we had not seen each other in almost a year. We spoke on the phone a few times, but our lives had taken other directions. It was nice, though, of her to call me, and the thought of seeing her made me uneasy. Would there be something still left between us? Perhaps, but she was with someone else, living in Paris, and I in New York. Long-distance loves do not last.

When we saw each other again, she was wearing a blue high-collared pullover and had cut her hair. Her smile was as irresistible as when we had met for the first time. We took each other by the hand and could not let go. I don't know what we spoke about. I know that we looked into one another's eyes and felt close. Coming out of *Sant'Ambroeus* we hugged. I had to go back to the office and asked her: "Would you like to have dinner with me tonight?" And this is how, without many words, our story continued. Anita stayed; she could no long-er leave. In those years New York was a violent city. People were leaving Manhattan, and apartments, and living, cost little and the air was filled with creativity. The city was not yet the place where one spoke only of money.

We lived a happy, carefree life and after a few months decided to get married. Anita was expecting a child and that was exciting. We were young and wanted to be together, have a family, live in America. We had little money and were renting a large room on Wooster Street in Soho, where artists were starting to live. The place was dangerous at night, but we paid no attention. Anita had read Dr. Leboyer's books on pain-free childbirth, and we decided to have the child following his method. Anita had started to work in fashion, for a French tailor, and opened a boutique. She nursed Sam, our child, and I was writing my first novel. After a year, a girl was born, and we called her Sole.

How long did our love last? There were crises, but we could not live apart and decided to stay together forever. We had our third child, Max. We had become a family, just as we had dreamt. Through the publishing house where I worked, I had established contact with Andy Warhol's *Factory* and with Fred Hughes, his manager. Together, we worked on a project with *Interview* magazine. In the end, the project came to naught, but they asked me to write for the magazine. One afternoon in *The Factory,* while Anita and I were talking to Bob Colacello, the editor of *Interview,* Marcel Pernod, a young, extroverted and gesticulating man, arrived. It immediately became obvious that he was eager to make a strong first impression on Anita and me, because he had taken a liking to us right away. Anita did not follow fashion. She had a particular elegance that preceded, by a few years, what would later become fashion. She had long legs and wore tight, high-waisted trousers. She had a passion for sandals. In very little time, Marcel Pernod became a close friend, especially with Anita. He would come visit us in New York and in the country. He wanted to be the favorite, and in a certain sense, for Anita, he was; but our life was filled with talented people coming and going, and that made Marcel, who wanted always to be the best, jealous. Every time we had a male or female guest, he either had to seduce or mortify them, because he alone wanted to be indispensable. Our children had become attached to that strange character who knew everything, who taught everything to everyone and would occasionally disappear to go and take drugs or fall in love with a newcomer. In those years, we had great fun in New York, stayed out until late in the evening, went to parties, to concerts. The years went by quickly and the children grew. They were American, athletic. Sole lived in her own world of fantasy and drew. We had moved and gone to live in the West Village. Anita developed a crush on Bill, who had a modelling agency, ate only hamburgers and lived glued to the television so that he would not miss a single game of tennis or basketball. In the fall, he'd go hunting in Pennsylvania. I had not paid too much attention to their relationship, because I was often in Europe for work. We neglected each other, took our marriage for granted, and things were collapsing. Marcel did not want us to separate because we had become his family. He kept warning us, trying to make us understand that we should not destroy our love because of little infatuations that were like passing clouds. It was true that we had neglected each other and that in recent years the children had been the main topic of our conversations, the children and not our love story. The argument that created the biggest distance between us was about Anita wanting our children to study in an American school and feel American. American in the way that Bill and Marcel were. I, on the other hand, wanted them to maintain their European roots, speak French, Italian, German. The difference of opinion was there because Anita had fallen for a real American like Bill, and I carried on a flirtation with a French woman whom I would see on my trips to Paris. Thanks to Marcel's insistence, things between us returned to the way they had been before and were even stronger than before. Bill became a friend to both of us, and the French woman and I ended things out of weariness. I had decided to travel less and used my savings to buy a small house on a Greek island. I wanted my children to know and love the Aegean Sea. They might be American, but I wanted them to have a strong tie to the Mediterranean. I wanted this because I am convinced that a human life is made of different layers. On the one hand, it is important to be pragmatic. If one has a good idea, it is fair to enjoy the success that one deserves. On the other hand, it is important to broaden one's horizons. To know the ancient world and the civilization of the past. This is why I had chosen Patmos, an island in the Dodecanese with a majestic monastery towering over it. It is said of the island that St. John had written *The Apocalypse* there. The monastery belonged to the Church of Constantinople: a sacred Turkish place on Greek territory.

I thought that the island, famous for its stony beaches where the light would sometimes be beyond beautiful, was a perfect synthesis of certain values that to me seemed fundamental. To be immersed in a landscape where the protagonists are the sky and the sea, where the blue of the sky and the blue of the sea melt in different shades at each hour of the day. Nothing is lovelier, more mysterious or more poetic than those long sunsets when the sea turns a kind of blue which grows more and more defined and the sky acquires pastel colors that range from blue to pink, red, yellow, and disappear into the fog. Looking at the landscape from the monastery one can see, far away, islands with names unknown, standing out like magic mountains, like vague forms appearing on the horizon. When the night comes, the moon illuminates the island. The sky is a cloak of shining stars, the moon a beacon of light. I asked my children to watch, for a long time, the sundown and the night sky and let it enter them like a memory to be kept forever. The island of Patmos, their secret place of meditation, anywhere in the world they may find themselves; knowing that one loves so deeply an Aegean island. A safe harbor where the civilization, the spirit, the earth, the sea and the sky are joined, and where the wind rules when he blows light or strong on tamarisks that grow behind the beaches and bend like pliant rushes. The island where the air is dry and where sometimes the wind brings with it dust from African deserts and leaves it lying on the beach stones. A simple, essential, gaunt nature. The animals that can be seen almost everywhere on the rocks and in the meadows are goats, the true rulers of the island. I wanted my children to take with them, in their hearts, that landscape and those values of an ancient and primitive simplicity. The values that are the extreme synthesis of the West and the East.

Anita had started to fall in love with the island and to take possession of it. For her, too, the island had become one of the places of her life.

Our children would grow up in America, go to university, each one of them taking up a different profession, they would get married, and Anita and I would become grandparents. But the passion for travel, for making new friends and exploring new paths would never leave us. Anita would spend a lot of time in a country house where children and grandchildren would come to visit. We had a little white dog who followed us anywhere we went.... Our marriage was a glue, the most important thing and it grew over the years, by now indispensable to our lives.

In reality, things had gone differently. I was sixty-two years old when I met Anita, one January in New York, where I was on a business trip. Through an Italian journalist friend, I had found an apartment to sublet from an elderly lady who was spending the winter in the Bahamas. I had Vladi, a young Romanian guy helping me, because I had a leg in a cast following an accident in London before Christmas. A female friend suggested that I get in touch with a French woman named Anita. According to this friend, the two of us had certain affinities. At that time, I was very lonely, and the idea of meeting a new person awoke my curiosity. I did not have the faintest idea of who Anita was, and no expectations. I called her one Sunday afternoon and asked whether she wanted to come and have lunch with me. She said she would come on Wednesday. To receive this unknown woman, I decided to wear something average – not too professorial, not too elegant, not too sporty – and chose a navy-blue fine-ribbed English corduroy suit. The apartment I was living in had a long corridor that led from the entrance to the living room. Since I could not move around because of the cast, I thought I'd wait for Anita seated on the couch and reading a paper, and my young helper would go and answer the door. At that time in my life, I was always tired, and had neither energy nor love affairs.

The most recent one, with an Israeli woman, ended badly when after a brief summer we had an argument, and she did not remain close when I had the accident. Instead, she went on vacation. The accident had scared me, and I was still in shock, taking many medications and having to go every week to have the cast changed.

I heard the doorbell ring. I was sitting on the couch, with the newspaper in my hand. Vladi went to answer the door. I heard footsteps, and Anita appeared: a tall, blue-eyed woman with large, fine hands, her face resembling women in Flemish paintings. It seemed extraordinary that fate had brought her to me. She knew about my accident, but we did not linger over my troubles. I immediately felt the need to tell her about myself. Intimidated as I was, I kept talking, telling her about my life. She spoke little and kept smiling, moving her long legs. She was wearing dark-brown leather trousers and boots. I think she had a white pullover on. The food was simple, but luckily, I had bought a good bottle of Sancerre. I don't remember how the conversation went, because the only thing I was thinking of was how to detain Anita for as long as possible. I felt close to her in such a strong and sudden way, and every now and then, when I would realize that she was about to say, "I have to go now," I would ask if she could stay a little while longer and I kept talking, ceaselessly talking. After lunch we sat down on another couch, and I caressed her leg. I think I told her that I loved her. She smiled. I tried to kiss her while we were saying goodbye. I would have wanted her to stay with me forever. As soon as she left, I felt an emptiness and, at the same time, an unexpected happiness. Who was this angel who chanced into my life?

We parted without a mention of another meeting, saying that we'd speak on the phone. After a few minutes, I was already missing her and would have wanted to call her. But I realized that in my enthusiasm I had exaggerated. I knew almost nothing about her. She told me that she had been married to Sulzberg, a famous pianist and composer. They had three children together but had been divorced for many years. She had recently left a German man. She had just returned to New York from Fontainebleau, where her ninety-nine-year-old mother, who had been in very poor health, lived.

I could not resist, and so I called her. I felt that the tone of her voice was different, more distant. I asked what she was doing the next day and if we could see each other. She said, "I don't know, I don't believe so," and I said "I apologize if I've been too impulsive, hasty, invasive." "Yes, that's right. You exaggerated." "I am sorry, I was emotional, forgive me."

A few hours went by and I called her again. She told me that she liked the fact that I had realized how exaggerated my behavior had been and had asked for her forgiveness. So we saw each other again. I don't know if it happened that evening or the next, but we made love and I was clumsy, awkward, with my leg and the cast. I think it was she who said, "Why don't you come over to my place tomorrow?" I did not know the West Village well, nor where she lived. I discovered that she lived in one of those tall, five-story houses that in New York are called *brownstones.* The house was close to Washington Square. Here I was in the New York of Henry James, of the American intellectuals of the nineteen-fifties and sixties. I remembered that my mother and aunt had friends in New York, the Abramsons, whom they had met in the Spanish and Portuguese Synagogue during the war. The Abramsons had a bookstore in the West Village. Who knows if that bookstore was still there? It was snowing in New York, and Anita had caught a chill. We spoke for hours, and she told me that she was not ready to consider a new relationship. Too little time had passed since her affair with the German had ended. She told me that she needed six months. I did not understand why six months, but my instinct told me that between us things would loosen up by themselves, day by day, and that Anita was only being cautious.

One Saturday I met Sole, Anita's younger daughter. Tall, with long hair, dark-brown eyes, an ironic, probing look, and a changing expression, she could act touchy and a moment later burst into laughter. From her elusive glances one could tell that she was a seductress. With Sole and her boyfriend, a young musician who would push my wheelchair through heaps of snow and mud, we stopped at a pet shop, and there I saw a skinny white puppy, with huge ears, all trembling, and bought it for Anita. She was surprised, curious, reticent. She did not want a dog, she did not know whether she wanted a dog. We called him Mario.

Bella, Anita's elder daughter, showed up late one evening, accompanied by a young man. She wore a coat made of Afghan or Indian cloth, seemed agitated and kept saying that the following day at dawn she would leave for India, where she was supposed to meet a guru. Bella had light chestnut hair and eyes that were light, brown and gentle, enthusiastic and dreamy eyes, poetic, melancholy. Anita's daughters were different and special. They resembled their mother but were less reserved. They were affectionate, intelligent, and insecure. They quickly accepted me as a friend with whom they could speak freely about their problems and their lives.

Early one morning, at eight o'clock perhaps, I was at Anita's house, in her bed. Anita got up and had gone downstairs to the kitchen to make a coffee. After a little while she returned to the bedroom and was no longer alone. Pointing to a person who had accompanied her upstairs, she said: "This is Marcel." A slim man in a silk embroidered shirt and a large yellow silk shawl resting on his shoulders, he started to speak profusely. He moved like a dancer, and gesticulating told a story about a certain Josephine and an island called Nives. He kept talking and talking, and I kept withdrawing further and further into my refuge under the covers and could not figure out whether I found this man amusing or frightening. But who was he? What was the point of this spectacle? Why was he speaking without interruption, in that sarcastic and tiresome, petty, and gossipy way about things and people whom Anita knew but I did not? I could hardly understand his American English, snobbishly peppered with French words. I saw that the man had a devilish glance, a horrible nasty tongue and sensed that it was better not to have him as enemy. Later I would find out that he was a poet, an artist, a heroin addict, a man with a peculiar taste who had been, for a while, a tutor to Anita's children and was her best friend.

I saw Marcel again: he would come to my apartment to chain-smoke Camels without filters, talking about art, people, artists, New York. Little by little I discovered that he had been born to an awful family, with an assassin of a father who beat him and who had been to prison. I would find out that he had shared an apartment with the poet Allen Ginsberg, and that he was the first one to have written about Jean-Michel Basquiat. In several rooms of Anita's house, there were watercolors with poetry written on the color with a paintbrush. They were by Marcel. He would spend his money, when he had it, on jewelry, drugs, books.

By now the six months that Anita had asked for in order to free herself from her love affair with the German had passed, and we were building our life together, day by day. She knew my children, my friends, I knew her friends. She felt a strong connection to New York, but most of her friends were, just like her, French expatriates. Marcel would come and go. Then there was David, an artist; Tony, an Armenian friend from her youth; Jean, an American friend, and Dominique, a French friend. That is how our life was becoming choral, increasingly made up of things shared.

In Anita's house there was much talk of the *bonne maman*, her mother, who was supposed to die any moment, but never did. And so, one kept wondering how to celebrate her hundredth birthday, assuming she did not die before. I would hear Anita speak on the phone with her sister Anne about how her mother had struck a nurse or sent away the maid or had a crush on one of the male nurses. He had said how fond he was of her, and she replied: "Yes, but at my age I can no longer do anything." Anita's mother was called Mary. I met her when I visited her small house in the middle of a park in Fontainebleau. She was a thin woman, with white hair, and after an accident she could only see in one eye. She would drink half a bottle of bourbon a day and ate many chocolates. She had been a riding champion, airplane, and helicopter pilot, spent the war working for the Red Cross, and, before marrying Anita's father, was the lover of a famous French general. Anita's relationship with her had been a conflicted one of love and intolerance.

Two lodgers lived in Anita's house. There was a Nigerian gentleman who lived in a basement room with no windows, and a small apartment on the fifth floor was occupied by Bill, a former boyfriend of Anita's, a sleepwalker with a big, deep voice who laughed loudly and always wore jeans and a white shirt. His rent money paid for Mercedes, a very lazy Columbian maid who kept saying "Miss Anita" and worked little. I had told Anita that I was irritated by the two grand pianos that belonged to Sulzberg, her first husband, and which occupied so much space in the living room. Signs of Sulzberg's presence were everywhere: sheet music, photographs, records, news-paper clippings, and every now and then Sulzberg himself coming to the house in the continuous comings and goings of children, children's friends, and lodgers. I had the impression of living in a bed-and-breakfast. People would come to talk, eat, drink, gossip. Even though we were in twenty-first-century New York, the atmosphere was like a nineteenth-century Russian novel. At any hour there was a stream of people with no plans, and there were several dogs, among them a bulldog and a chihuahua, besides our little white dog with huge ears.

When Anita and I went to Italy, to my family's old country house near Turin, Marcel came to visit us from Vienna. He took to the house right away, and turned the library upside down, grabbing books and taking them with him to his room. He would cut roses in the garden and make bouquets together with my helper Vladi, who was a good-looking young man and to whom he felt attracted. He accompanied Anita to town to look for antiques – crystal vases, small porcelain objects, jewelry – or they would go and visit museums. It seems that in the Egyptian Museum, with his constant objections and corrections, he drove the woman director mad, who was guiding them through a collection. Marcel did not stay with us for many days, but he left a strong memory of his presence. After the summer, I did not see him again. Only in December did I find out that he was very ill and had been hospitalized. In Turin he pretended to be suffering from diabetes, when what he really had was a tumor, one or more metastases, and did not have much time left. He had no money, and they no longer wanted to keep him in the hospital, because he could not pay. Anita and Marcel's other close friends organized, and they wondered what to do and how: Who would pay for him? In the end, Anita decided that if Marcel had to leave the hospital, she would have him stay at her house. In the meantime, she went to see him every day. She was a great cook and would ask him whether he wanted something special prepared, and then she would take it to him in the hospital. There were many conversations and phone calls between Marcel's friends and between Anita and her daughters, who worshipped him and contended for the position of his best, closest, most cherished and intimate friend. I knew that Anita was the divine woman, the muse that he looked up to with love and admiration. The year before I met her, he had accompanied her to Portugal, where they had visited museums, churches, bought porcelain and tiles... Marcel was attentive to Anita, and she would say: "It is special to visit museums with him. He explains everything to you, knows everything, makes you understand and see things that you'd never see without him." Marcel and his talent, his culture, his wriggles, his rages, his weaknesses: he was a myth that I had accepted.

Marcel died on the night of January thirty-first, in the hospital. It was extremely cold outside. The news took Anita by surprise. She had gone to visit him the day before and did not think that he could die so quickly, a few hours after they had talked, laughed, and joked together.

The preparations for the cremation and the funeral began. Who would organize the ceremony? Who was supposed to make a speech? Who would pay for the cremation, the flowers? What kind of flowers could one find at that time of the year that Marcel would like? A competition of sorts was unleashed over who was Marcel's greatest friend, a kind of rivalry. Anita decided to invite Marcel's friends to a dinner at her house and to drink champagne in his honor.

Around the table, the friends told stories, episodes. Anita spoke little. That death, expected and unexpected, was causing her pain. A difficult, on occasion unbearable, man had left her life, nasty but a genius, and no one would be able to replace all those years that connected them, all the memories. Marcel inspired fear in many because he could not be controlled, and his sharp tongue could strike, like a serpent, at any moment. He would feel a sudden, exaggerated, passion for a stranger, or a terrible, unjustified hate. But with Anita it was different, because she kept him at bay. It was she who inspired fear in him, and not the other way around. It was she who punished him and kept him at a distance when he would go too far.

The morning of the ceremony at the funeral parlor, Marcel's friends followed one another: young, old, friends from the past, the present, artists, poets, publishers, dealers, muses, his Spanish widow. Many among those present, including Anita's children, one after another, came to the podium to say a few words or read a sentence, or a poem, in memory of Marcel. Anita remained at her place. She did not want to make a show of herself, because there were no words to describe her feelings. Her daughters spoke for her. When the ceremony was over, a big discussion ensued about what to do with the ashes: who would have to keep them? One of Marcel's brothers showed up at the funeral parlor, with a nephew. They looked like simple Americans, dressed in an ordinary way and behaving normally. The nephew was a son of another one of Marcel's brothers, who had killed someone in a bar with a rifle. They hardly knew Marcel and felt like strangers in the world of artists who had come to commemorate him.

The ashes and the urn that contained them ended up at Anita's house, where in another small box, on a shelf in her workroom, she kept the ashes of her father, to whom she had been very close. I wondered how come she was not troubled by the fact that a friend who had spoken to her just a few hours earlier had become a small heap of ashes placed in the basement of her house between the stored suitcases and the room where Mercedes ironed clothes. But Anita was a woman who rarely showed her emotions and her thoughts, because she preferred to hide behind a childish smile. She could appear brusque on occasion, or too busy.

On the other hand, when she talked about something that interested her, or was close to her heart, she would gesticulate to express with greater emphasis what she wanted to say. It was difficult to define Anita as either a cheerful or a sad woman, because she would go from very happy laughs to distant silences. In some cases, she could appear haughty, but she was shy. After Marcel's death she would share that grief with Sole and Bella.

She had a different relationship with her son Lev — more exclusive, more intimate than with her daughters. They told one another nearly everything and helped one another. Theirs was a strong, special kind of love. He had trust and admiration for his mother, and she adored that handsome, athletic son who reminded her of her father. The girls were jealous of that relationship: he was a man who worked, earned money, and excelled in sports. Anita was glad to be loved and admired by her children. She had always lived with them and for them. Each one had in their possession one or more of Marcel's paintings, and Marcel was constantly quoted and remembered. Anita was more restrained; she didn't enjoy remembering. Perhaps in her silences she hid thoughts that she either did not want to or could not express.

The relationship between Anita's children and Marcel, who had taught them to understand the world of art, culture, and music, had been strong and useful in helping them, not always successfully, to face the difficult relationship they had with their father, a self-centered, arrogant man, preoccupied only with success and the relationship with his woman-of-the-moment. In the center of everything was music, and when he was in love with a new woman, something that happened to him frequently, everything would revolve around her, and the children had to adapt to the new arrival, humor her until the love affair would come to an end. Then, he would become depressed and would draw the children into his despair, venting his feelings in front of them. But as soon as he met a new woman, he would become detached and think only of her, and everything would begin again as before, until the love affair broke off again, and Victor fell out of euphoria and into despair.... The children felt insecure in that fluctuating relationship, because when Victor was depressed – either because of his failures or because he felt abandoned – he would grow closer to one of them, temporarily misleading them into feeling that they were the favorite one, only to push them away as soon as a new love came to be. This did not mean that Victor was a bad man who did not love his children. He was simply incapable of thinking of anything else but himself and would abandon himself to his moods, his passions, careless of others' feelings. Only his son Lev had managed to take a different, less dependent, attitude.

Sometimes amused and sometimes less so, Anita listened to the stories that her daughters would tell her about her ex-husband. They spoke a lot about him and suffered because of his behavior, which they judged to be disgraceful. Yet they loved him deeply. At times, I would become irritated when I felt that Victor was occupying too much space in our conversations. At one point, exasperated by the excessive number of pianos, records and other things that would invade the house with his presence, I bought an ancient harp and placed it in in a corner of the bedroom to mark my own presence.

Marcel's ashes stayed at Anita's house until the brother and a sister, whom no one had met before, made the claim that they were supposed to rest in a cemetery in Massachusetts, next to their mother. There was a long conversation about those ashes and that ceremony, until Anita and Sole, one cold, rainy morning got into the car and took the ashes to Massachusetts.

I was certain that Anita and Sole had each taken some ashes from the urn to keep for themselves. And I was right. I found out, in fact, that a small heap of ashes ended up in a small white-and-blue porcelain box that Anita had bought when she and Marcel had visited Portugal together. Another small heap ended up in another small box, kept by Sole.

As months went by, I saw that despite the very strong memory of Marcel, Anita's sadness was waning, and that she was becoming used to his absence. Sometimes she would say: "It is incredible: Marcel knew all the books he had read by heart. He was like a living encyclopedia."

One evening Lev spoke with Anita and me about Marcel: it was clear that he had exercised a formative` influence on him of the kind that his father had not. Lev, speaking of Marcel with affection, told us that as a child, in order to defend himself from his invasive and at times annoying presence, he had bought padlocks to lock his room with a key. Lev recognized in Marcel a real talent: he had been the one to make him understand art and music, worlds Lev was biased against because of his father. As a child, Lev was very close to Bill, who was then his mother's boyfriend. Bill encouraged him in sports, had him meet tennis champions, basketball and hockey players, took him hunting and to baseball games. He taught him what a real American man is. Bill could have been a character in a Hemingway novel. Sometimes I wondered how two people as different as Marcel and Bill were able to live in the same house, around Anita and her children. But they understood one another because, between accidents and violence, both had experienced a tragic and lonely childhood. They had lived in the world that Carver speaks about in his stories, or Capote in his *In Cold Blood,* the violent world of O'Neill's comedies. Each one of them was American in his own way and played a different role in life.

A few months after Marcel's ashes had been taken to Massachusetts, Anita and I went to Fontainebleau for Mary's hundredth birthday.

Mary was in a good mood, and I asked her many questions about her past, about her time in Paris, the war years, the general she had been in love with. She talked to me about her husband and told me that he had a lover who, like her, went riding, but Mary would always beat her in horse races. Every now and then, Mary would laugh and then say, "I am *gaga,* I don't understand anything anymore!" At one point, I asked her what was the thing that she desired the most, and she, without hesitating, said that she was hoping that Bella would get married and have a child. She said that with enormous love. Mary was living alone, with her dog, an inseparable dachshund, Cesare Augusto. In the afternoon she enjoyed going out with Cesare Augusto, driving her golf cart in the woods that surrounded the house. Sometimes she would stop and doze off. Every day she read the *New York Times* and watched television. She amused herself by ridiculing the butler at her sister's house, who colored his hair and moustache tar-black and, like a peacock, kept driving his blue Jaguar back-and-forth around the property.

The celebrations of Mary's hundred years were memorable. The only surviving sister came with her daughter and several grandchildren. The daughters had lovingly organized a lunch at the golf club, and she was happy. She was laughing, delighted, at the head of the table, and the bizarre hat that Bella had found for her, half fairy-like, half queen-like, fit her head like a crown. Everyone was cheerful, proud to be celebrating that grandmother, that mother, that aunt who was so very old. The celebrations lasted for days. Mary lived on for two more years, with highs and lows, her daughters' worries, changes of nurses, maids, and doctors.

One day, while Anita and I were in Madrid, her condition took a sudden turn for the worse, and Anita had to leave immediately to join her sister in Fontainebleau.

After she died, Mary was cremated, according to her wishes. On a rainy afternoon in November I attended the funeral. Speeches were made, videos were shown. After the ceremony there were refreshments that lasted a long time, where everyone talked and drank. Mary's was a large family, and all the cousins, in spite of the occasion, were happy to see each other again.

We would almost never speak of Mary again, and Anita and her sister no longer had to worry. With Mary's death, the European root of their life had disappeared. They would no longer have that small house lost in the garden and the woods, where they had become used to visiting Mary in recent years. Anita spoke little of her pain and grief for the death of her mother. I had not asked myself where Mary's ashes had been laid, but I found out that those that were due to Anita and her children had been divided. For several months, they remained in our bedroom in the house close to Turin; and afterward, during a summer we spent on a Greek island, they were dispersed into the Aegean Sea, because Mary had expressed as much. Bella also kept a small heap of ashes, and one morning a year later, in Greece again, Anita told me: "I have to accompany Bella to find a cliff, a beach from which to throw into the sea the ashes that had remained of my mother." I continued to find it terrible that one spoke of this so lightly, and that unbeknown to me, for several months, the ashes had remained in a small box in our bedroom.

At this point it seems appropriate for me to say that something concerning my death has changed.

Ever since my paternal grandmother had died, I had known that at Montparnasse, in Paris, there was a family grave where my grandparents and my father were buried. The Paris grave, where seven places were still available, was for me an important point of reference. Not only because on Yom Kippur I went to place stones on the grave and recited the prayer for the dead, but because I knew that this would be my last home and that I would be buried there forever. Besides, I could not be buried in my mother's grave, because there are no places left. I sometimes think that me not going often to Paris is not important, because I will end up there forever anyway. Anita came with me to my father's grave more than once, but she wants to be cremated, like her father and her mother, and has not decided if all her ashes should be deposited in one exact place or dispersed, or whether to divide them in three for her children and, in that case, arrange for three equal boxes, so that there is no injustice. A curious thing about dividing ashes is that one does not quite know what is being divided. In other words, if one dissected a cadaver, one could say: the head to you, the heart to me, the legs and feet to you, and so on. Or one's organs can be donated for medical use. Be that as it may,

Anita wanted to be cremated, and I to be buried with my father. I was almost certain that my children and their spouses and children would come to my funeral, but then I was not sure that they would come to visit me, not because they were not affectionate, but because they cannot always stop by Paris. Once I am buried, five places will remain in our grave, but my sister is entitled to three and therefore I am left with only two. Seeing that I have three children, there is no space for everyone, unless I reclaim the three places that belong to my sister. In any event, I have lived longer than sixty years, and at least forty in the quiet certainty that I would end up in our Paris grave, but this year something peculiar happened. Hélène, my father's wife, my sister's mother, died. We were fond of one another, and I have to say that although her death was foreseeable, because she was ninety-seven, I was hoping that like Anita's mother she would live to be at least a hundred years old. Unfortunately, that is not how it went: one February night she died in a Paris hospital. I managed to see her the night before, but at five in the morning a phone call informed me that she had died a few minutes earlier. I did not want to wake up Anita, who was sleeping, and I left our hotel room on tiptoe, took a cab, and in the deep darkness of the city still asleep, I arrived at the hospital. I found the room where Hélène was lying cold, immobile, lifeless. Her face was marmoreal, with an unfamiliar expression. Her features had dried out, leaving a strong dignity on her face. Twenty years earlier I had found myself alone in a room at a clinic, with my dead father, and now I was alone with his dead wife. To be alone in a room with a dead person can give rise to different feelings. One is in shock, because one never expects death. The dead person is no more. The body is cold and the life, the soul, is gone. The dead body seems the same as before, but the person is no longer breathing, no longer seeing, no longer hearing, no longer moving, no longer speaking. The person who is there before us is no longer with us. The body is with us, but not her thoughts, her reactions, her feelings. That person will be no more, will no longer speak to us, no longer think. That person who wanted, felt, spoke, did, imagined, is forever gone. But because of this, seeing that the body remains, I cannot understand letting oneself be cremated. The ashes are powder, they are the cancellation, the annihilation not only of the soul, but of the body. I disagree with Anita; I find it proper that the dead body should slowly disintegrate and become a skeleton. At least that skeleton is ours, these are the bones that have held us together, that allowed us to move. One says, "flesh and bones," but the bones remain and fossilize. I might be told: "But of what importance is it that the skeleton be preserved? What counts is that the children, grandchildren, houses, works of art remain." Perhaps so, but one spends one's life taking care of one's body, following diets, exercising, doing sports, and then all has to end in dust?

That January morning, I watched Hélène, my stepmother, immobile. Until a few hours earlier, she had smiled at me, talked to me, complained of the cold, and then she was no more. I could shake her, scream, sing, touch her feet, caress her, pull her hair, tickle her, but she would not react. Her body was there with me, I could speak to her, tell her all I wished, but she was dead and could not hear me. A few hours later, Hélène would be laid in a casket and buried close to my father. I would join her when my turn came. On the face of my dead father I had seen relief: he had died to free himself from an atrocious illness that had struck him and that, day by day, devoured him before our eyes. Hélène had a gaunt, distant face, as if by dying she had wanted to withdraw into her thoughts. After the funeral I asked my sister: "What do we do about the grave, who will take care of it?" She replied: "I found out that my mother had a legal right to the grave, and now that right has passed onto me. Just think, before dying you will have to ask me for permission to be buried." The fact that she was telling me with a jocular and amused tone that the grave was hers, or at least under her jurisdiction, was an enormous blow. But how? I would have to ask for permission to be housed forever in that grave that I thought ours, my final home? My sister attributed no importance to that purely bureaucratic matter, while I thought about it a great deal. It was certainly not her fault, and not even the fault of her mother, if things had gone this way. This was something that depended on the law or a statute, yet I felt betrayed. Betrayed in my thinking, because my certainty of being buried in Paris was no longer there. I became aware of this sudden insecurity when Anita told me that her mother's ashes, as well as her binoculars, were still there in the bedroom of the Turin house. This is how I too started considering the possibility of being cremated, but when I spoke about it to Elie, a dear friend, he told me: "You needn't get cremated. If you want, I can give you a grave in Jerusalem."

"Because... you have graves?"

"Yes, for me, my wife, my parents who are already buried there. But I have others, and I also gave one to Lord

Samuelson, who died a few months ago and is buried there."

"You know that in a few months I am going to spend some time in Jerusalem?"

"How come?"

"I am going to teach."

"Ah! Very good."

"I could go and take a look at the grave."

"Yes, go, but with someone, because it is dangerous."

"So why should I get buried there if it is dangerous?"

"If you're dead, it is no longer dangerous. Not like in certain European countries, especially in France, where they defile Jewish graves. Sure, if you'd like to feel safer, you could get yourself buried in America, although, as you know, there is a strong rise in anti-Semitism at American universities."

"And in Switzerland I'd be safer?"

"I don't know. I don't know Swiss cemeteries, although I should, considering that I am Swiss, but I don't fear danger and I'll be close to my parents in Jerusalem."

It is a pleasant thing to think that a friend wants to give me a grave, but if it is dangerous, assuming that my children and grandchildren want to come and visit me, it is not a good idea. Seeing that I was no longer certain that the grave in Paris was mine, although I knew that my sister would immediately, without hesitation, grant permission to bury me there, I began to think that I could buy myself a place in the Jewish cemetery in Turin, next to my mother, my maternal grandparents and Primo Levi, whose grave was just next to my mother's. Yes, I could have rested between my mother and Primo Levi. I spoke about this topic, which was beginning to torment me, to one of my children, who in turn was thinking about not having a grave and needing to acquire one. But if we had constructed a family tomb at Turin cemetery, I mean for me, the children, the grandchildren, I would have wanted to choose an artist or an architect to design it. I could give a gift of a grave to my family, but not be buried with them, because in Italy the cemeteries are divided by religion, and I will have to be buried in the Jewish section of the cemetery, and not in the Catholic one. For the love of family and in order for us to remain united in death, too, I could convert at the last moment, but I am against conversion. Religion depends on God, so if one is religious one obeys the will of God. If He wanted us to be born of a certain religion rather than of another, He must have had his reasons, his designs, and therefore to convert, in my view, is going against God's will. I am not a believer, and once dead, given that I do not believe in the afterlife, what does the religion matter? Better to be Catholic and buried with my children than being Jewish alone. But I would not be alone if I bought myself a grave close to my mother and Primo Levi.

Anita did not give me advice on this. She was very discreet, also because as far as she was concerned, everything was simple and clear. No celebration, life ends, and then we turn into dust. What fascinated me about her think-ing was that she, once dead and therefore no longer being Anita, did not want there to be traces of her dead body. She had been what she had been, there were photographs, portraits of her over the years, she had children, and her voice had been recorded, and therefore there was no lack of evidence of her having been on this earth. Anita had been but was no longer.

Her soul was a different topic. Though she had spent much time in India, in contact with Eastern religions, I am not saying that she believed in reincarnation, but perhaps she thought that her soul would transmigrate.

The idea that my soul was supposed to transmigrate did not convince me, because if after me or before me it could belong to anyone else, this made me think that my life was just a passing through and that I was a temporary renter of that soul. Besides, it is said that the world has to come to an end, and with it the human beings, and so everything that has been constructed over the centuries is useless and will collapse: scientific discoveries, pyramids, works of art, books, religions, countries, families. Nothing will remain. I realize that the ashes are not a wrong choice, because it is our will to make disappear, to dissolve that which we were. This way our body will belong neither to the worms, nor to the birds of prey, nor to the wolves. We were that body that carried us forward, made us breathe, walk, run, swim, make love, reproduce ourselves. That body will not transmigrate anywhere, not even the brain that made us think and dream. I was telling myself that it would have been better to decide to become dust before the world explodes and mankind ends. The afterlife had fascinated the Egyptians, who made a cult out of it. They would prepare their immortality with great care and attention to detail, through the graves, as if once dead, transformed into mummies, they were to continue to live the way they had done in life. According to certain religions, our soul will go to hell, purgatory or paradise.

Death therefore is a reward or a punishment, and that too is a way to drag life out, a way of thinking as living beings, with the divisions into the good and the bad. But what preoccupies me is not my soul, because I do not quite know what it is, and whether it is a part of my body or not and therefore whether it ends with my death or whether it belongs to a power or a supreme will that will do with it as it pleases. No, I can only decide what to do with my body after my death. I can decide what I want for my funeral, how to be buried or whether to be cremated. Then there is the matter of euthanasia, whether I have the right, in the case of extreme illness, to refuse heroic treatment; but that is a technical or religious matter and I admit to not having thought much about it, even if I know that this is a serious mistake, as it is a mistake not to think of senile dementia or Alzheimer's. What should one do in that case? Where should one spend that time of life scatter-brained and absent from the life of others? With a brain gone mad that no longer responds? I had not thought about that, either. I had not yet thought of how I would die and how I would react in case either my brain or certain organs of my body failed. I needed to hurry and write up my will.

By now I was almost seventy years old. I worried about my death, about where I would end up. Of course, I enormously disliked thinking about that, instead of continuing to write every day, wondering what to eat, looking at the sky, swimming in the sea, breathing the mountain air, reading a book or seeing a film, I would become a simple tiny heap of ashes. I was thinking how the voice would vanish into nothing; the conversation would stop and sensual and sexual pleasure would disappear. I would fall asleep without dreaming and without waking up, and Anita would no longer be next to me. I would not be able to ask her: "Did you sleep well?" She would not reply: "And you?" I would not tell her: "You know, I had a strange dream." I would not look out from the window to find out what the weather was like. Anita would not ask me: "Would you like a tea or a coffee?" I would not be anxious to check if an e-mail had arrived, if I had a bill to pay, if we had enough money. I would no longer speak to my children and tell stories to my grandchildren. I would become, for each one of them in a different way, only a memory. Was I afraid of their judgment? No. I knew that we had always loved one another. And our dog? That small white dog, Mario, who had followed us everywhere, slept with us, licked us early in the morning to remind us of his presence and his wish to go out? That gentle-looking dog, who barked and sometimes bit certain strangers who would bother him, or whom he did not like – would that small dog realize that I was no longer there? Would he slip into my side of the bed, would he take my place close to Anita? After a period of mourning and emptiness, she would become attached to another man, but I could not imagine which one, because throughout her life her taste had been eclectic. She could fall in love with an American musician or an English lawyer, or with someone younger than she who would make her laugh and make her feel young. Would she remember me? Perhaps with the man who would enter her life she would occasionally speak of me, of us, of our relationship....

The Egyptians used to prepare for their death in great detail, because in the certainty of immortality they organized their graves as if they were their houses, taking with them everything they had used in their lifetime. What would I have taken with me, had I been an Egyptian? If one could read, I would have taken the *Odyssey*, the *Divine Comedy*, *War and Peace*, and other essential books. I did not know if in the tomb I would be aware of the change of hours, seasons, or climate. But supposing that everything remained as it is in life, I would have taken with me pens, felt-tip pens, pencils, pencil sharpeners, notebooks, reams of paper, in case one could continue to write. I would have taken shirts, pullovers, trousers, socks, handkerchiefs, shoes, suits of different weight, a blue coat and a beige coat, a windbreaker, two scarves, two wool berets, a few photographs, *Leckerli* marzipan cookies that one can find in Basel, long-lasting breadsticks, *fontina* cheese, and dried salt beef. The dead do not eat, and yet the Egyptians would take food to their graves. Marmalades, carobs, bread. But if there really should be an afterlife, similar to the life one had while living, being cremated is like committing suicide. To prepare for one's death is something the living do, and everyone can arrange that transition in one's own way.

I don't know why, but just when I was thinking about this, one of my grandchildren told me that he did not believe in God, because religion, and therefore God, are a human invention, and that the Bible is an absurd story which does not make sense. His is a logical reasoning, a bit like with Santa Claus: one believes in him as a child, and then no longer. Santa Claus is an invention for children; God and religion are an invention for every age.

When one has an obsession, one always lives with an ear pricked up for anything that reminds one of that obsession. The other day, for example, I heard someone speak about a gentleman I had known, who had always lived half with his wife and half with his mistress, and it was said that the wife had behaved with great style when the family met in Venice for the funeral, during which the ashes were to be scattered in the lagoon. The wife had asked that the mistress be present, too, seeing that she had shared one half of her husband's life. So, they divided the ashes between the two of them, and each one, with great composure, scattered her part. With a body this would have been impossible; there would have been too many arguments. Yes, since the ashes are anonymous, we do not know whether the small heap that we are taking was the liver, the brain, or a foot. On the other hand, assuming that it were possible to cut a body in two, it is not possible to divide it in an equal way. In other words, of a body one can divide in two only that which is double: two hands, two eyes, two arms, two legs or two lungs. But if one were to divide in two, for example, a foot, one for you and one for me, there would in any case be injustice, because one is the left and the other the right one. The right hand, in my case, given that I write, is more valuable than the left one; and if I were a leftie, the opposite would be true. No, there is no doubt: the ashes are simpler and more rational. It is like cold cash compared to properties and objects. It is more likely that one ends up fighting about common properties. But the fact remains that in the end one has to decide. I should have written in my will what I wished my heirs to do with my body. In his will, my father left practical and moral instructions on how the funeral was to take place, who was to take part in it, who would say the prayers, and so it was done. For my mother it was simpler: she knew that she was the only one who could be buried in the family grave, and that after a troubled life she would return close to her parents, far from the two husbands and the children. My father was certain that he would end up next to his parents and that his second wife would join him. I was to join him later. But to the very end, fate has denied me the certainty of that burial, and Anita and other circumstances made me wonder about the possibility of cremation. That said, it is true that if I decide in favor of the ashes, everything is much simpler, both for myself and my children. Besides, I can decide to leave to each one of them, and to my grandchildren, a small heap in a tiny box and ask that the remainder be scattered at a place of my choosing. If, on the other hand, I can no longer go to Paris or have a new family grave in Turin because of the differences in religion, then I need to choose a place especially dear to me. If I want relatives and friends to come and visit or say a prayer, it is better that I choose a place easy for everyone to reach; but if I prefer to be left in peace, and am not particularly concerned whether they come to visit or not, I can find any place that holds a special meaning for me. Anita thinks that my reasoning is macabre, and that I should think more about how to live my life with her instead of organizing my death. She is right, but seeing that the place I choose for my burial will be definitive, it is right to be certain about it. For those who do not believe in resurrection, the only certainty in life is death. Death, which is the biggest mystery of all. Life, my life, is like that of everyone else around me, and it will end.

In the meantime, I am alive, I travel on a plane and think about Anita and our relationship. We are almost always together, we talk, we caress each other. She wants, absolutely and forever, to be my only woman; I need her, need not being without her. Her absence scares me; I am afraid of her and I need her. I could not say and describe what we say to each other or do together. We live and talk, mixing realities that are sometimes boring, memories, plans.... Travel plans, life plans. And then we fight, we're jealous. We are also boring, because we repeat to one another things and stories that we've told each other a thousand times. Anita moves her hands with surprising agility and when she touches mine, I feel her; sometimes I look at her from the front and from the back and find her special, sometimes I do not pay attention. She loves to discuss, understand, analyze, believes in psychoanalysis and in yoga. I sometimes think that she loves me in a violent and possessive way.

Other times in a gentle, tender and occasionally brusque way; other times she seems to me impatient, distant. We speak of our past, of our loves. It is curious that Anita, who very much loves objects and possessing works of art, should wish to be cremated and become dust, while I who love neither objects nor possessions am looking for a grave.

I was struck by a story a friend shared with me. Her grandmother had told her that she had prepared two identical coffins lined in light blue, in two different cities, because she would die either in Paris or in Florence. Then she changed her mind about the color of the lining and had the light blue removed and replaced by a burgundy fabric. One evening when she was in Paris, she phoned her granddaughter to tell her: "I am going to die tonight." She died, in fact, that night in Paris and was buried there. I did not know whether, besides two coffins, she had also planned for two graves.

Anita did not want to own a grave. But did she really know what she wanted? Did I understand her and know her? Her moments of closing-up, her silences or certain impatient words made me afraid; sometimes I wanted to leave, end our relationship. But then things would go in a certain way and everything would be as if nothing had happened. As if there had been no inside storms. One begins to write a story and does not know how it will end; one begins a love story and does not know how it will end. There are incomplete works and incomplete love stories. Life, on the other hand, begins and ends. There are no incomplete lives, because even those who commit suicide do not have an incomplete life. They interrupt their life by themselves, like a writer can tear up a manuscript. After having thought about my death, and particularly about my grave, about where to be buried, and not having reached any conclusions, I now have to think of the time that I have left to live. But it is not that easy to free oneself from an obsession, because there are odd circumstances that take me back to thinking about it. I received a message from a female friend that said: "The priest has left! Just call me." I called, because I knew that she was not well and jokingly told her: "What were you doing with the priest? Making a confession? Was he giving you the rites?"

"No, he came to tell me about my son's ashes, because he says that I can no longer keep them at home."

"Is it a sin for a Catholic to be cremated?"

"Yes, I think so, and this is why the priest came to talk, but I cannot stand priests."

"What do you want?"

"To keep the ashes at home, and later scatter them in the sea."

"You told me that you had kept the ashes in your boyfriend's office."

"Yes, but he's no longer my boyfriend, and so I brought them back home. And as you can imagine, in the small village where I live everyone knows everything about everybody, and someone spied on me, because they found out that I was taking the ashes home. The priest came over right away to tell me that I had to take them to the cemetery and that I could not keep them at home. But I'm keeping them at home anyway."

I have never asked her why she had decided to have her son cremated. I knew that for her it had been a terrible tragedy, and that she had felt guilty.

I remember that when they called to tell me that Alberto Moravia had died, I was in Paris, in a café at the Place Saint-Michel, the *Café du Départ*, and I immediately left for Rome. When I saw Alberto in his coffin, which had not yet been closed, he was wearing a navy suit and a red shirt with white stripes that I had given him, and a pink silk knit tie that I had bought him in America, at the Harvard Coop. He loved that tie. He had lost it during a trip to Yemen and asked me if I could buy him another one. A few weeks later, he told me that a hotel-keeper had found it and sent it to him by mail. So, Alberto was buried in a shirt of mine and a tie that I had given him. I asked who had dressed him; I was told that it was the undertakers. No one knew about my shirt and my tie; it was a secret between me and Alberto. This is why I do not like the idea of the ashes: because they have nothing accompanying them in the way that the body has. Alberto died, but they dressed him in my clothing. Christians do not allow cremation and dress the dead with elegance. Jews are buried with the *tallit* of the son or the father.

Would Anita and I remain together forever, as she said? But that forever does not mean for eternity, because, unless souls really exist and are able to rejoin one another, something that would greatly surprise me, we will not be buried together. She will be cremated and her children will take possession of her ashes; they will divide them and so on, while I, sooner or later, will have decided where to be buried.

Sometimes I would like to settle down for good in a village, change my name, disappear, and think about my life and its meaning. It seems absurd to continue talking with Anita, about what will happen after death. Her idea of turning into ashes has a flicker of freedom in it. It is like saying: "I'll be thrown into the sea, into the desert, onto the mountains and no one will be able to own me!" Yes, because there will always be vandals, barbarians, racists, Nazis who will desecrate graves and cemeteries. There will always be men and women with horrific values, the frustrated ones who will use physical and verbal violence, hate towards the others. There will always be envy, malice, betrayal, sadism. The world of the good and the bad. By having ourselves cremated and our ashes spread, we prevent others from owning us. What has been has been, and that's that. There are things about cremation that are horrible. The ashes, for example, destroy the DNA, so it can no longer be established whether one is truly someone's legitimate or illegitimate child. Terrifying stories have been heard and known about people who had themselves cremated immediately after death, so that their illegitimate children could not be recognized, but this is a sordid aspect and I prefer to think of a poetic aspect. We are born and live in society, our lives are like travels, routes, stories that end with our death. Certain people have contributed to the culture, science, inventions and discoveries, and some discoveries have changed the destiny of human life, changed the very human beings and their habits, but then? As long as we live, the fear remains that something bad could happen to us before we reach death. We fall in love and encounter one another. Anita lives with me, I live with her. Sometimes we do each other good, other times we hurt each other. Being alone is different from being together. There is something like a sense of belonging, of being rooted in life with its highs and lows and its uncertainties; together we have a territory, a house, dishes, books, friends, memories, experiences. A friend told me: "I like poetic women." Poetic women are those we love, because poetry is what best describes in words the feeling of love. Music and poetry evoke that deep and unexplainable feeling that is love. Love that makes us live and makes us suffer. Love that does not exist in concentration camps, because, as Primo Levi writes, with every trace of humanity annihilated, man is to be reduced to mere thoughts of surviving and not dying. The slightest distraction means dying. In a concentration camp life is only fear, suffering, horror, annihilation of values, struggle not to end up in the ovens of the crematorium. What makes us bear life in the most terrible moments is the fear of death, the fear of being no more. Except for extreme moments, one lives guided by hope, curiosity and life itself. One lives because there are instincts. Never mind that when I am dead Anita will become ashes: for now, she is flesh, muscles, bones, kisses, caresses. To be alive means to laugh, cry, be afraid, sing, scream, whisper, exist, be timid, be a show-off. As long as there is life, Anita will have that laughter that is very much her, strong, indifferent to being labeled. She loves sauces, pickled fruit, cabbage, cucumbers, garlic, octopus, sea urchins, eggplant, fennel, and cooked celery. She likes cappuccino, vodka, white wine.

I hope not to die soon because I'd like to see my grandchildren grow up. I am curious to find out what kind of adults they will be, what they will make of their lives. I don't know what will happen in history, if racists, fascists, those who do not want freedom but only fear and injustice, will return to power. Perhaps one day, replacing little by little all of one's organs, one will end up never dying. But the soul? What will happen to our soul, to that *flatus* we have inside? The intelligence, the talent – where do they come from? Who has decided that our soul has to remain in our body? What difference is there between the soul and the body? Are they the same thing? Is love an example of the soul and the body? One is attracted by the body, the eyes, the voice, the lips, the gestures, by something that strikes us, that captivates us. Sometimes one falls in love and one's legs shake; one's stomach closes up. Are these physical reactions linked to the soul? Is falling in love soul or body? Is being jealous soul or body? The body gives continuous signals, chills, psychosomatic pains. Anita would like me not to be a hypochondriac, but what can I do? Being afraid of illness has to do with the feeling of fragility. It is true that we can climb the highest mountains, explore the bottom of the seas, construct pyramids, bridges, skyscrapers, planes, but we are fragile. Our fears come from the body, from the soul, from many different things. Anita seems not to be afraid because she never complains. But I know that she is afraid of abandonment, of being abandoned. I have not figured out whether she is afraid of death or whether she is repressing it. It scares her to love. She believes that she knows this fear, a fear that comes from long ago. The fear of that which cannot be controlled, the fear of losing, of feeling defeated.

Yesterday evening, while a young and talented pianist was playing Ravel in the sitting room of a private residence, I thought that to die means to abandon one's friends, life, music. Leaving the house where the pianist had performed, a blonde woman of an uncertain age, whom I had shortly before heard being called "the richest woman in America," something that always makes a huge impression in America, said to me: "I found the caviar sandwiches they served before the concert to be exquisite. The dinner was good, too, and they say that the cook had two stars!" After having spoken in this way, with great simplicity she climbed into an Aston Martin station wagon, a rare car, and smiling, said goodbye. Great wealth, luxury, power, all things that will end with life, but which remain a point of arrival, a dream during one's life. If it were not for that need to dream that there are people with exceptional destinies, kings, queens, billionaires who live unreachable lives, human beings would be different.

As long as one is alive, is there anything lovelier than gossiping with friends on a sunny morning in a café, over a cappuccino with brioche, or a Campari soda with toast? Life is serious, frivolous, superficial, tragic, sad, terrible, marvelous, but then it ends for everyone. The Earth is for rent; others will follow later, and we won't know anything of it. To be remembered, one has to leave a trace of one's passage. Usually the most remembered are tyrants: Cesar, Louis XIV, Napoleon, Hitler, Stalin, or a few heroes like Churchill or Gandhi, some artists, scientists, athletes. The others will die leaving only their children, who in turn might pass through without leaving a trace. Like pawns, stories of soldiers dead on battlefields, peasants dead of exhaustion, workers reduced to robots.

Anita and I talk a lot about our life, our relationship. Every day, we wonder about the mystery that is keeping us together. Love. And what is love? Love is a feeling, a chemistry, a memory, a habit, a dream, a smell, a music, a photograph. When one of my grandchildren tells me on the phone: "Grandpa, I miss you." That is a deep, true feeling: a grandchild, a grandfather, the common thread of life. He is the one who continues after me, after his father. Life is a chain that lives on until it breaks, until the family dies out.

Joel and Veronique, two of Anita's friends who had recently weathered a crisis, came to her house in the country. Paul, their eight-year-old son, was with them. Joel is an adventurer with long, blond hair, a large aquiline nose and small, cunning, vivacious blue eyes in permanent movement. He makes you laugh, laughs himself, is ironic, pretends to be distracted. She is very much in love, beautiful, younger than he, from a good provincial bourgeois French family. She paints, he sells paintings. Theirs is a great erotic attraction. Joel is a child of poor parents: his father used to beat him with a belt, the mother was a cleaning woman in a café. He and his brother grew up as hooligans on the streets of Nice. The brother was killed by drugs; he managed to escape. At the table he said that he was an atheist and that he prays to God only if they put him in handcuffs or if he runs out of money. I asked him: "So you do believe in God?"

"No, I pray to him in extreme circumstances, because you never know."

I asked him: "Will you be buried or cremated?"

"No, not cremated, I don't like it. I want to be buried somewhere difficult to reach. I want it to be difficult to come and visit me."

"And where?"

"In Antigua, my island. It is the place to which I feel most attached. If one goes there and asks about me, everyone remembers. I used to drink two or three bottles of rum a day, took cocaine like mad, had a bottle of Valium in my pocket if I felt my heart bursting."

"Have you quit?"

"Yes."

"Do you miss it?"

"No, but every day I have to look after myself, the way one looks after one's diabetes."

"With what medications?"

"I attend a daily meeting and then, one needs the will. Sometimes, if I do not go to a meeting, I become nervous, short-tempered. Drugs are an ugly beast, it is something you have in your head, and only you can make it go away."

Later I asked Anita if Joel was a real friend and if one could trust him, and she said yes.

And then, with the enthusiasm she shows when she likes to talk about a subject, she told me where Joel came from and how important Veronique had been in his life, helping him to leave the small world of dirty business and drugs in which he had been living for so many years. At the table, when Joel said that drugs were a tragedy and that his brother had died of drugs, for a moment he became emotional. When they left, I told Anita: "I think that Joel is a sad man." She said: "I don't think so. He is a nice man who takes life with irony and humor." I think that people who laugh a lot, who make others laugh and are always quick on the draw, are sad.

At times I wonder how one can continue to live when people around us who are a part of our life begin to die. When in June, Catherine, a dear friend of Anita's, died, I felt a profound sadness. Another person was leaving the life of Anita, who had a short while before lost Marcel and her mother. Catherine was not cremated, but buried in a Jewish cemetery on Long Island, next to her husband. Anita, although she did not believe in funerals, said: "I am going not so much for her, who is no longer here, but for the people around her, who loved her, for her children. A few weeks before she died, Catherine asked: 'Come quickly'. I went and we spent time together, but I should have gone earlier and been closer to her." I felt guilty for being an egoist. For not having understood that I should have encouraged her to go before; but something had tormented me. A mixture of pain and jealousy. Before the inevitability of the death of a person I love, I withdraw, I am afraid, I am afraid to see the person suffer and I am afraid of how my life will be without her. Afraid of the void and the fact that the person will no longer be here. A memory, of course, remains, and the dead often return to our mind, and if they are no longer with us, they are our past. We can no longer phone one another, have coffee, go to the movies, gossip!

Today my sister called to tell me that she took care of our grave. She said that I had to send documents to the funeral director. I have to prove that I am my father's son, and fill out some forms. This piece of news pleased me, because I realized that my sister had understood my preoccupation and decided to help me reclaim my lost place. On the other hand, it seems absurd to me that in order to be able to have access to one's own grave, one should have to face a bureaucratic procedure.

I had lunch with a writer friend who works in New York. We talked about our writings, and he asked me: "Have you made progress with your book on Primo Levi?"

"No, for the moment I've set it aside, because I've had another idea."

"I've also set aside what I was writing. I don't like it anymore."

"I am writing something that is neither a diary, nor an essay, nor a novel: it is a *thing*. It is as if I no longer had the desire to write novels."

"I no longer feel like writing novels either, you know? Sometimes they are just stories to distract the reader from his daily thoughts. What are you writing?"

"Something about my death, about death in general, on how to be buried, cremated or not cremated. It is a serious problem that concerns us all, that has concerned all civilizations."

"That's right, ever since the Etruscans! It is a problem I had not thought about until a short while ago, but lately I've thought it over. I understood that I did not want a grave with a monument, but I don't know whether to be buried with my parents or whether to think of a grave with my family: my children, my wife."

"I can see that we have similar thoughts."

I told him my story and said that I am undecided whether to make the effort to reclaim my grave in Paris and set my soul at rest, no longer to think about it until my death, or whether to forget about the bureaucratic procedure and make another choice.

I have a friend, Bob Margolis, a poet from St. Louis who, after having studied at Harvard and lived in Boston, settled down in New York, where he lives alone in an Upper-West-Side apartment. Bob publishes in the most prestigious and influential cultural magazines. He is a poet in the tradition of Pound, Auden, Lowell. He likes custom-made suits by a renowned London tailor and Ducati motorcycles. I very much love Bob's warm, amused, and friendly laughter. Every time we meet, he asks me to come and live in New York, to move, and he advises me to write in English. I try to explain to him that it is difficult to leave Europe and write in another language. He almost never leaves the Upper West Side and always says that he needs to work. He spent too much time with women, drank too much, and now that he is eighty years old, he feels an urgent need to write. He reads the newspapers, watches TV news, and in the evening goes down to eat in the Greek restaurant on the ground floor of his building. He is passionate about politics, speaks French, and likes Italy. He helped me when I was in crisis, when I found it too difficult to live at Anita's house, when I felt nostalgia for home, for Europe. Bob is bald, not too tall, and he wears white shirts and chinos in the summer. In a restaurant he orders a Caesar salad or a salmon tartare. When we meet, he lets me speak, and I tell him about my vicissitudes. I talk to him about my work, about Anita, about one of my son's problems. He listens to me and calls me *my boy*. He does not give me advice, except to go and do physical therapy with a woman friend of his at Columbus Circle.

The dinner to celebrate Bob's eightieth birthday, held in a New York club, was lovely and moving. His closest friends came. A few lifelong male and female friends, his children, and his sister, whom I had never met before. Even though Bob is not religious and had children with a Protestant woman, in his own way he has preserved the Jewish habit of keeping the family united.

I had dinner with him at Luxembourg Café. He was in an excellent mood because he had finished a new book that would come out the following spring. We spoke about Anita and the way that, in his view, my life has considerably improved since I've been with her. While he was eating and drinking, I thought about how at over eighty he was still young and vivacious, and how he is a serious man who loves to laugh. A man who knows well how to recognize what is important. I am not sure that he is very happy to be living alone, and I did not dare talk to him about death, even less, ask him about where and how he wished to be buried. I would have liked to know whether he had decided to be cremated, but it did not seem right to ask him about it.

Bob is frank, poetic, direct. He has a strong work ethic. I have always been fascinated by those who do something concrete and become good at what they do. Death is the end of work, of one's craft. The craft, the work, are life.

At the end of September wet leaves fell on my car, forming yellowish stains. I took the car to a specialized garage, close to Southampton, to get it cleaned and have the stains removed. There, a blond young man with a bit of a paunch, gray-green eyes and a hat, was assigned by his boss to remove the stains from the body of my car. He asked if I spoke Spanish, because he was Columbian and did not speak English, and he did not care much to learn English, because he did not like being in America. I asked what his name was. He answered: "Alex." While he was beginning to clean the body with a large green cloth rag, spraying a blackish liquid, I noticed that leaning against a wall of the garage was a carbon racing bike, and asked him: "Is it yours?"

"Yes, it is extremely light, but I also have an Italian one, a Bianchi. I've been to Italy and raced. I love the Alps, the mountains. Do you bike?"

I lied and told him: "Yes, I do." His face opened up in a large smile while he continued, with meticulous patience, to try to remove the smallest possible stain from the body of the car.

He told me: "You'll see, the car will be sparkling. The boss asked me to do things in a certain way, but since I like you, since you're like a friend, I'll apply a special, more protective gloss.

I thanked him.

He asked me: "You know who my idol is?"

"No," I said.

"It is Pantani! I don't drink and I'm healthy. My only vice is the bike. Pantani used to drink, but he was a great man."

I asked him: "You like soccer, too?"

He made a grimace: "No, I don't like it, it's a game of many against many. The bicycle is one against all." After having set aside the cloth rag for a moment, he added: "I like it when it hurts here, in the thighs, when you feel that you are making an incredible effort."

"Right," I answered.

The car seemed shiny to me and perfect. He made me touch the body and said: "Feel how soft it is! If you were a regular client, I'd say that I'm done now, but as I said, I see you as a friend, and now let's apply another gloss. Americans come in, pay and never speak to you, they want you to be done right away, in a hurry, they're in a rush. But I like precise work done well."

Once the second gloss had been applied, and the car carefully polished with different types of rags, I told him: "Thanks, you've done a fine job."

He did not pay attention, but opened the door and polished it on the inside, took out the mats, brushed them, and put them back.

I told him again: "Thanks, really a fine job."

He did not listen to me and took another rag and another lubricant, and he started to clean the tires and the rims with extreme care. I admit that I could no longer take it; his professionalism was wearing me out. But how could I interrupt his zeal and his work? Actually, this was not his work, because he had told me that he had studied at the university, that he was a veterinarian. He also told me that, although he preferred to move around on a bicycle, he owned a Mini Cooper and a BMW. But then, why was he cleaning the car, caressing it with his gloves as if he were caressing a woman's body? I thought that this was the secret of life: whatever you're doing, doing it well.

During the days that preceded Yom Kippur I went to Paris to take care of my grave and of the necessary bureaucratic procedures. I am now determined not to be cremated, but to work on being buried in Paris. At the graveyard, I chose a stone for my father, one for my grandfather, one for my grandmother, and one for Hélène, who was buried next to them a few months ago. But while I was placing the stones down and starting to recite prayers, I noticed that Hélène's name had not been engraved next to those of my father and my grandparents. How come? I told my nephew Pierre about this. He said that he had noticed the same thing and that he had spoken about it with his mother. My sister told him that the name can only be engraved a year after one's death.

On Yom Kippur I went to the temple and sat down in the place that had belonged to my grandfather, and then to my father. Few of the people who had known my father had remained in the synagogue, but every year on Yom Kippur I feel the need to go. Hearing those voices, those prayers recited in the Ashkenazi Alsatian rite makes me feel good. That's when I feel Jewish and try to repent for my sins. I repent before God, but above all before myself. What I love the most is to fast and to be swept by the religious rite, and by the music that I've known since childhood, to listen to the rabbi reciting the Avinu Malkeinu, the beautiful prayer that closes the fast, followed by the sound of the Shofar.

The next day I went to the office of funeral services where an employee reassured me, telling me that the paperwork I had given him was all in order and sufficient for me to ask for an official permit to be buried in my family grave. I needed that official permit for my emotional balance.

In recent months, I've thought a lot, perhaps too much, about death and ashes. But I was not prepared for what happened.

In a text message, Anita told me that for her it was too late. She wrote that she wanted me to be her king so that she could be my queen, while I believed that she did not want to be my queen, because she is a free woman. I did not understand that Anita had real-life plans with me and I made her suffer in many different ways. I betrayed her with another woman because I had not understood that she wanted to be my queen, let alone that I was a king. I had preferred to seek refuge in the uncertainty of the solitary and melancholy life that had been my life as a child, when I lived alone with a governess at the *Pensione Europa* in Turin. I did not succeed in remaining in a relationship that could have been a happy, romantic, secure one; a positive, meaningful relationship. I was not able to understand the gentleness of a love shared and strong, because I feel the nostalgia for a life lived day by day, where everything is still possible, a life where you are always hoping that something unforeseen will happen, where you dream other imaginary lives, where you suffer because you are waiting for a message, a reply, a phone call, a rendezvous; a life where you want to find someone who loves you to bits, but you do not realize that there is Anita who really loves you. You do not realize this, because you are afraid of stopping, because the reality is not a dream and because you know that you are close to death. Anita asked me, in many ways and with many tears, to become the man that she wanted me to become, to become capable of reassuring her. But I feel nostalgia for the child who was not reassured, who was afraid and did not feel wanted and accepted; so I took life as a game, sometimes difficult and sometimes beautiful, and wrote stories because I was not able to make plans or build things. I live like a nomad, with one sole certainty: that of being Jewish, writing in Italian, and living in a world where English is spoken. My children and my grandchildren are the backbone of my life, and I've tried never to betray them. They will be the ones to judge me. I would like to be able to become or be what Anita is asking of me, but I cannot erase that inner feeling of desperation, that emptiness that sometimes makes me experience life as an unbearable burden, but which is also a deep, secret happiness. Writing this I understand why Aharon Appelfeld has been so important for me. Because, after living for sixty years in Jerusalem, he still thought in German, and he still felt nostalgia for the Carpathian Mountains. His nostalgia was similar to the music that I feel inside of me when at the synagogue they recite Yom Kippur prayers. I am capable of helping, but not of reassuring; I can only reassure a child, one of my grandchildren when he is desperately crying because he feels hurt, unloved, abandoned. The sadness of a child makes me want to cry, because it is an extremely profound sadness, one that I know well and still feel today. Anita wanted to be with me for the rest of our lives. I was afraid: what if she died? And what if she fell in love with someone else? I was afraid of loving her completely. When she discovered that another woman was in my thoughts, Anita grew desperate, and her world came tumbling down. She cannot believe that I can have other women besides her. It is a humiliation, a terrible wound. I was not capable of promising what she wanted. So one day, she decided to leave me. She preferred to defend her pride, not to accept what she could not accept. Now she is gone; I am left behind in the house that we wanted for the two of us and I am afraid. Afraid of not knowing how to live without Anita. We spoke, and I told her that the day after she left, I received in the mail my "official permit to be buried" in the Montparnasse cemetery. I asked her, if I die, will she come to place a stone on my grave, and she said yes.

Meeting Anita was very important. I feel it deep inside of me, and it hurts, yet I was incapable of not ruining everything. I had to see her leave to understand how much her absence was making me suffer. I did not understand that it was too late. I should have embraced her, kept her close, asked her to teach me how to make her feel my love for her, but something prevented me from doing that, and I let her go. It is true that we were very happy on a Greek island, in the azure of the sky and the sea, but now I'd like to go with her to a mountain village and walk. Walk as one walks on the clouds, without thinking about the many practical and social things that prey on ours and everyone's lives.

Perhaps for Anita I felt a different kind of love, and I understood that when we were in her mother's little house in Fontainebleau.

Now that I've examined all the reasons, right or wrong, why we could not be together, now that she is far away, I think of how many things we have done. She believes in astrology, in psychoanalysis, and wants to get to the bottom of whatever she's looking for. I would like to be able to be at peace with what I am living, without always looking for something else. Will I be able to force myself to accept that in life things can go well and that a certain happiness can exist without us being punished? I don't know. I think that I should walk for a very long time, learn about gratitude, the desire to help others, get out of my mad narcissism, not be afraid. Anita's departure has left an empty space in my heart. I did not think that she would have decided to end our relationship. For some time, she will think about us, about me, about what happened, and then the distance will do its work, and she will find another path. The same friends, but another life. She packed two suitcases and left our world. I sent her two messages, I tried to talk to her to say: "Wait. Perhaps we were wrong, one should not ruin everything, we still have time. Let's try again." I don't know why I needed to destroy Anita's heart. Why did I want to punish her, and only punished myself? How many times could I have started afresh with her, but did not want to do it.

Anita went to America to build a life for herself, her family, and I wanted her to come back to me and return, as her mother had done, to her origins: Europe. I wanted her to experience the same feelings as I. She told me she wanted to come and stay with me, and I did not believe her.

I know that Bob Margolis will be sorry when I tell him that Anita left, because he had asked me, advised me to try to be with her and not let her go. For many months I have thought of death, of what should be done with me after I die, and for the time being I've only secured a place for me at the Montparnasse cemetery, in Paris, next to my father. This is neither very creative nor very original, but my fate is to occupy the place next to my father, which has been denied to me during my lifetime, and which I hope will be granted to me in death. I was not able to live my childhood next to my father; he was my idol, my role model, but was unreachable and inspired fear in me. He was too beautiful, too important. Everyone called him President. He had many women, was a golf champion, loved beautiful clothes, shirts, pyjamas. He lived in luxury and had luxury cars, sports cars. He smoked a pipe or cigars, and wore a black hat and a blue coat. He inspired fear in me because I did not live with him and did not do well any of the things that he did. We did not understand one another and spoke little. I knew little about him and he little about me. We did not succeed in building a real relationship, but he was my father, we had the same last name. In death, I would like to be next to my grandfather and my father.

The doctor called me, worried about the results of my medical tests. There was something suspicious. I had to spend the entire day bouncing between clinics, laboratories, medical doctors. The result remains to be seen, but I felt a great fear. The fear that everything was about to end, and that from being free and healthy I could, from one moment to the next, become prisoner to the disease. No longer knowing what my fate was. Searching for myself, analyzing myself, hoping, letting out a sigh, being racked with anguish. Becoming, in the eyes of others or of those who love you, a sick man, a person who is no longer normal. How to live with the illness? How to prepare myself to leave this life? How terrible, thinking that all that we are will no longer exist. Even if I am cured, if I get better, I will not be the way I was before. How long do I have left to live? Am I prepared for this? No, not yet. The idea that all the ups and downs with my grave have been resolved is a relief. At least I know where I'll end up. The family will call Rabbi Sebag from the synagogue de la Victoire, who will come to recite the prayers and say a few words about me, appropriate for the occasion.

I am different today, I feel suspended. I don't know what the process will be like: will I be healthy and therefore exonerated? Will I be ill and therefore condemned? And if so, what should I do? Today is a day of a vacation from normal life, full of worries and feelings of unease. Should I be thinking about this? Should I forget? I have no desire to be ill and I want to die only when I am really old, in my sleep, without knowing it, unexpectedly.

I am in Jerusalem, in the lobby of the King David Hotel, where some American Orthodox Jews are having tea. This morning I was in Tel Aviv, where I rented an apartment because Anita wanted to stay in Tel Aviv, and we had decided to meet there. She was supposed to arrive from New York; we wanted to make a final attempt and see if things could be mended. But while I was getting ready to go and pick her up at the airport, I got a message on my phone telling me that she wasn't coming. I tried to write to her, to call her, but she did not reply. I felt a sharp pain in my back, in my chest, as if I had been stabbed. I had not expected this, and I began walking to and fro in the empty apartment rooms, like a zombie. Every now and then I would lie down on the couch. I had not shaven, had not yet washed. I stared at the ceiling as if it could help me or give me advice on how to behave. In fact, I realized that I was looking for God. I wanted God to tell me how to behave, what to do. Around eleven I called a female friend who lives in Jerusalem and told her: "I am coming to see you." I took a cab from Tel Aviv to Jerusalem, directly to the Wailing Wall, because there I would know better how to speak with God. I have never come to Israel without placing a prayer at the Wailing Wall. I am not religious, but ever since my childhood, I've felt the presence and the need for God, the need to turn to heaven to search for an answer. I felt alone in front of the Wall, but experienced an intense happiness listening to Orthodox Jews, with their black hats and black coats, reciting the Kaddish. That same Kaddish that I used to hear recited in Paris on Yom Kippur, that same Kaddish that Rabbi Sebag will recite at the Montparnasse cemetery when they bury me.

In front of the Wailing Wall in Jerusalem I did not ask for anything. I only wrote the names of my children and my grandchildren on a small piece of paper that I folded and inserted into the Wall, among so many other notes. Then I placed my hands on the Wall, which is the only symbol of Judaism that remains, and I recited the benediction of the kohanim for my family. Then I went on foot along the city streets up towards the Jaffa Gate. I crossed the Arab quarter, the quarter with the Holy Sepulchre, and the Armenian quarter. Walking, I felt nostalgia, sadness, because I had walked the streets of Jerusalem numerous times with Anita. Four years earlier we had come here for a few months. It was as if every stone, every place, every shop made me think of her. Walking the streets of Jerusalem, I felt that something strong tied me to this city, to these different religions, to the bells, to the prayers. A city ruled by religions, which were all wanted and founded by men, but it is as if in Jerusalem the presence of God were watching over all of them, since He is the God of all religions.

Anita will be cremated, and her ashes scattered in a place of her choosing. I will go to Paris, into my father's grave. For now, our destinies have parted, and after so much talking what one needs is silence. And this is how, in silence, in Jerusalem, this story ends.

London, February 2018

About the Author

Alain Elkann is an author, intellectual, and journalist who was born in New York and grew up in Italy. Of international fame, he is the author of more than thirty books many of which have been translated into numerous languages, including French, Spanish, Portuguese, Russian, Hebrew, Turkish, Japanese, and English. His many awards include the following: Premio Cesare Pavese, Premio Internazionale Tarquinia-Cardelli, Premio Capalbo, Premio Letterario Mondello-Città di Palermo, and the Premio Acqui Terme.

Since 1989 Alain has maintained a weekly interview column for the Italian newspaper *La Stampa.* He has addressed an impressive range of celebrated subjects, including award-winning writers and editors; film stars and directors; fashion designers and businessmen; artists, collectors and museum curators; politicians and diplomats; economists and historians; thinkers and human rights activists. Two books of his more intriguing interviews have been issued by Bompiani, with whom he has published the majority of his books.

A recurring theme in his writing is the history of the Jews in Italy, their centrality to Italian history, and the relation between the Jewish faith and other religions. He has lectured on art, Italian literature, and Jewish studies at the Universities of Oxford, Columbia, Jerusalem, and Milan's IULM. He is a member of the Board of Guarantors of the Italian Academy for Advanced Study in America, Columbia University. He is President of The Foundation for Italian Art & Culture (FIAC) in New York.

About the Translator

K.E. Bättig von Wittelsbach teaches in the Department of Romance Studies and Jewish Studies Program at Cornell University.

CROSSINGS

AN INTERSECTION OF CULTURES

Crossings is dedicated to the publication of Italian—language literature and translations from Italian to English.

Rodolfo Di Biasio. *Wayfarers Four*. Translated by Justin Vitello. 1998. ISBN 1-88419-17-9. Vol 1.

Isabella Morra. *Canzoniere: A Bilingual Edition*. Translated by Irene Musillo Mitchell. 1998. ISBN 1-88419-18-6. Vol 2.

Nevio Spadone. *Lus*. Translated by Teresa Picarazzi. 1999. ISBN 1-88419-22-4. Vol 3.

Flavia Pankiewicz. *American Eclipses*. Translated by Peter Carravetta. Introduction by Joseph Tusiani. 1999. ISBN 1-88419-23-2. Vol 4.

Dacia Maraini. *Stowaway on Board*. Translated by Giovanna Bellesia and Victoria Offredi Poletto. 2000. ISBN 1-88419-24-0. Vol 5.

Walter Valeri, editor. *Franca Rame: Woman on Stage*. 2000. ISBN 1-88419-25-9. Vol 6.

Carmine Biagio Iannace. *The Discovery of America*. Translated by William Boelhower. 2000. ISBN 1-88419-26-7. Vol 7.

Romeo Musa da Calice. *Luna sul salice*. Translated by Adelia V. Williams. 2000. ISBN 1-88419-39-9. Vol 8.

Marco Paolini & Gabriele Vacis. *The Story of Vajont*. Translated by Thomas Simpson. 2000. ISBN 1-88419-41-0. Vol 9.

Silvio Ramat. *Sharing A Trip: Selected Poems*. Translated by Emanuel di Pasquale. 2001. ISBN 1-88419-43-7. Vol 10.

Raffaello Baldini. *Page Proof*. Edited by Daniele Benati. Translated by Adria Bernardi. 2001. ISBN 1-88419-47-X. Vol 11.

Maura Del Serra. *Infinite Present*. Translated by Emanuel di Pasquale and Michael Palma. 2002. ISBN 1-88419-52-6. Vol 12.

Dino Campana. *Canti Orfici*. Translated and Notes by Luigi Bonaffini. 2003. ISBN 1-88419-56-9. Vol 13.

Roberto Bertoldo. *The Calvary of the Cranes*. Translated by Emanuel di Pasquale. 2003. ISBN 1-88419-59-3. Vol 14.

Paolo Ruffilli. *Like It or Not*. Translated by Ruth Feldman and James Laughlin. 2007. ISBN 1-88419-75-5. Vol 15.

Giuseppe Bonaviri. *Saracen Tales*. Translated Barbara De Marco. 2006. ISBN 1-88419-76-3. Vol 16.

Leonilde Frieri Ruberto. *Such Is Life*. Translated Laura Ruberto. Introduction by Ilaria Serra. 2010. ISBN 978-1-59954-004-7. Vol 17.

Gina Lagorio. *Tosca the Cat Lady*. Translated by Martha King. 2009. ISBN 978-1-59954-002-3. Vol 18.

Marco Martinelli. *Rumore di acque*. Translated and edited by Thomas Simpson. 2014. ISBN 978-1-59954-066-5. Vol 19.

Emanuele Pettener. *A Season in Florida*. Translated by Thomas De Angelis. 2014. ISBN 978-1-59954-052-2. Vol 20.

Angelo Spina. *Il cucchiaio trafugato*. 2017. ISBN 978-1-59954-112-9. Vol 21.

Michela Zanarella. *Meditations in the Feminine*. Translated by Leanne Hoppe. 2017. ISBN 978-1-59954-110-5. Vol 22.

Francesco "Kento" Carlo. *Resistenza Rap*. Translated by Emma Gainsforth and Siân Gibby. 2017. ISBN 978-1-59954-112-9. Vol 23.

Kossi Komla-Ebri. *EMBAR-RACE-MENTS*. Translated by Marie Orton. 2019. ISBN 978-1-59954-124-2. Vol 24.

Angelo Spina. *Immagina la prossima mossa*. 2019. ISBN 978-1-59954-153-2. Vol 25.

Luigi Lo Cascio. *Othello*. Translated by Gloria Pastorino. 2020. ISBN 978-1-59954-158-7. Vol 26.

Sante Candeloro. *Puzzle*. Translated by Fred L. Gardaphe. 2020. ISBN 978-1-59954-165-5. Vol 27.

Amerigo Ruggiero. *Italians in America*. Translated by Mark Pietralunga. 2020. ISBN 978-1-59954-169-3. Vol 28.

Giuseppe Prezzolini. *The Transplants*. Translated by Fabio Girelli Carasi. 2021. ISBN 978-1-59954-137-2. Vol 29.

Silvana La Spina. *Penelope*. Translated by Anna Chiafele and Lisa Pike. 2021. ISBN 978-1-59954-172-3. Vol 30.

Marino Magliani. *A Window to Zeewijk*. Translated by Zachary Scalzo. 2021. ISBN 978-1-59954-178-5. Vol 31.

Lightning Source UK Ltd.
Milton Keynes UK
UKHW012029191121
394266UK00001B/22